I0762844

The Evil Garden

by Edward Gorey

aka Eduard Blutig

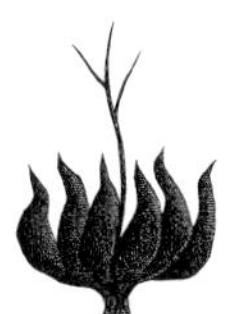

Pomegranate Communications, Inc.
105 SE 18th Ave., Portland, OR 97214
800-227-1428 pomegranate.com
sales@pomegranate.com

To learn about our newest titles and special offers from Pomegranate, please visit pomegranate.com and sign up for our newsletter. For all other queries, see "Contact Us" on our home page.

This edition first published by Pomegranate Communications, Inc., 2011.

Library of Congress Control Number: 2010937848

Item No. A195
ISBN 978-0-7649-5885-4

Printed in China

34 33 32 31 30 29 28 27 26 25 21 20 19 18 17 16 15 14 13 12

The Evil Garden

Eduard Blutig's Der Böse Garten
in a translation by Mrs Regera Dowdy
with the original pictures of O. Müde

Alas, my translation of perhaps Herr Blutig's most famous work appears on the melancholy occasion of the seventy-fifth anniversary of the next to the next to the last time he threw himself out of a window.

MRS R.D.

How elegant! how choice! how gay!
To think one doesn't have to pay.

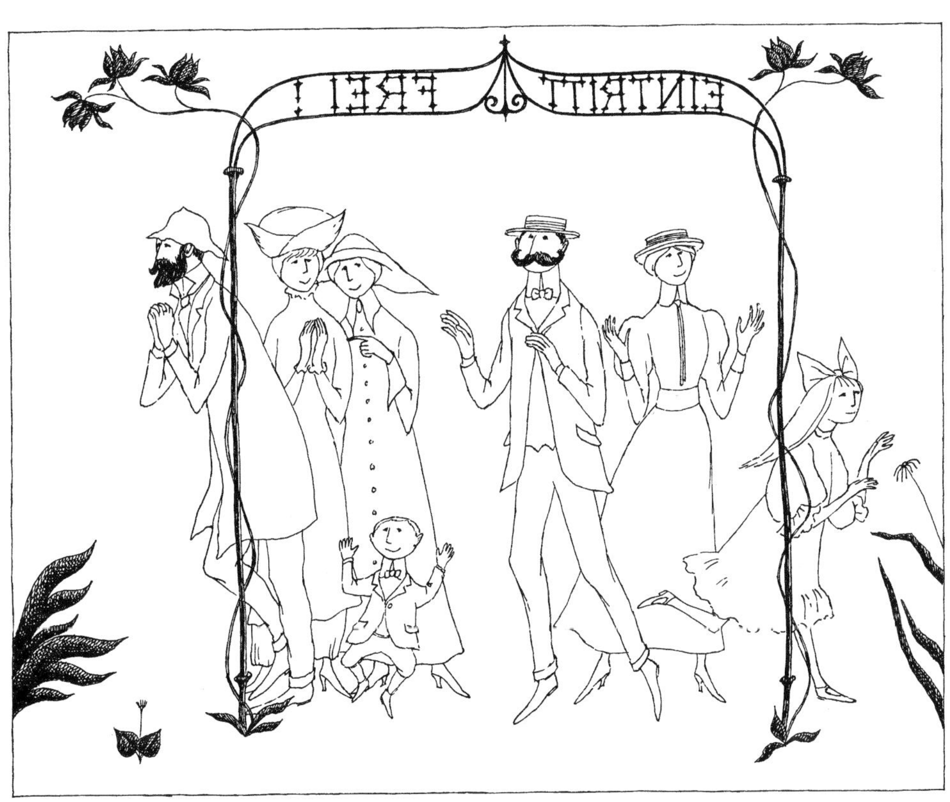
EINTRITT FREI !

There is a sound of falling tears;
It comes from nowhere to the ears.

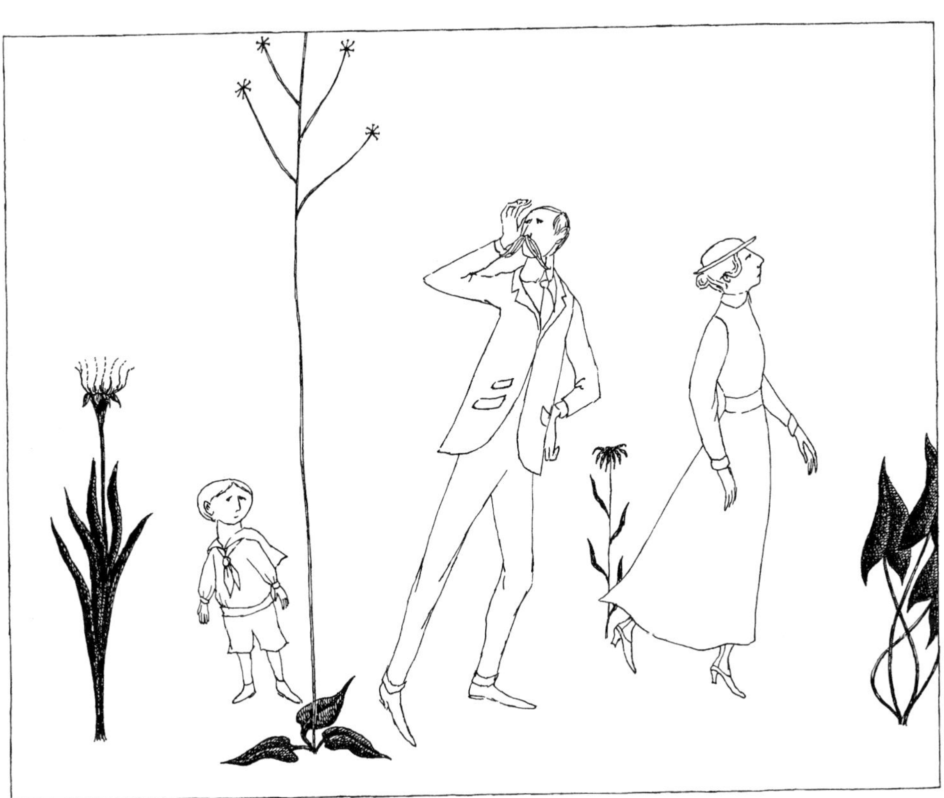

Some tiny creature, mad with wrath,
Is coming nearer on the path.

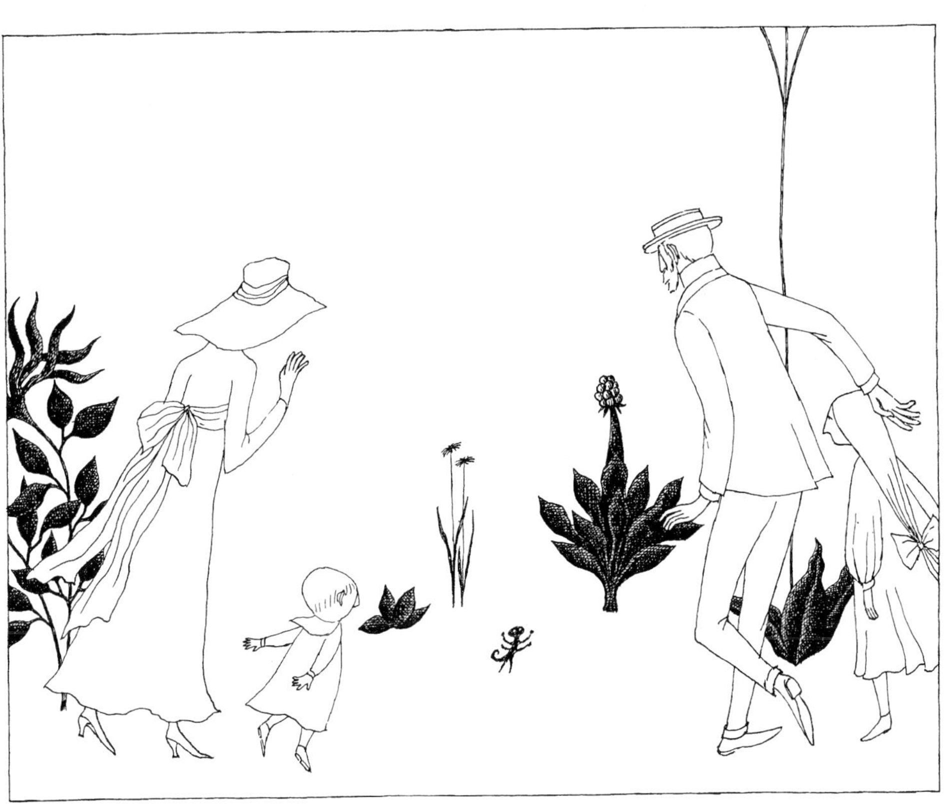

A foot inside a stripéd sock
Protrudes from underneath a rock.

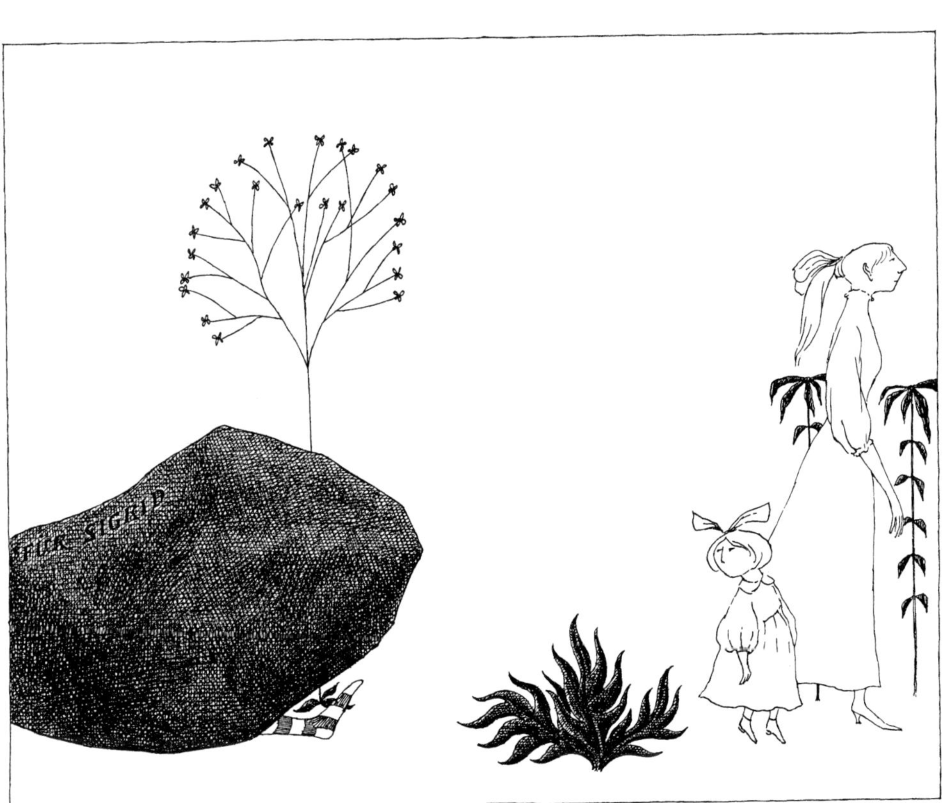
SIGRID

The gorgeous flowers have a smell
That causes one to feel unwell.

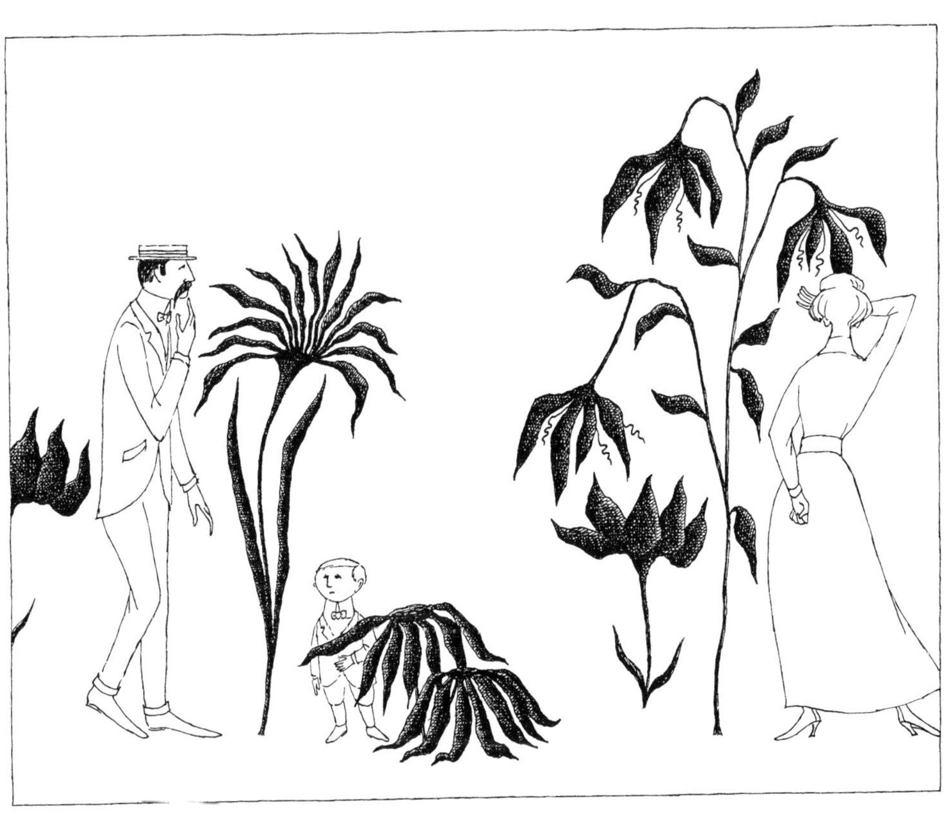

The Rev. Mr Floggle's cloth
Is being nibbled by a moth.

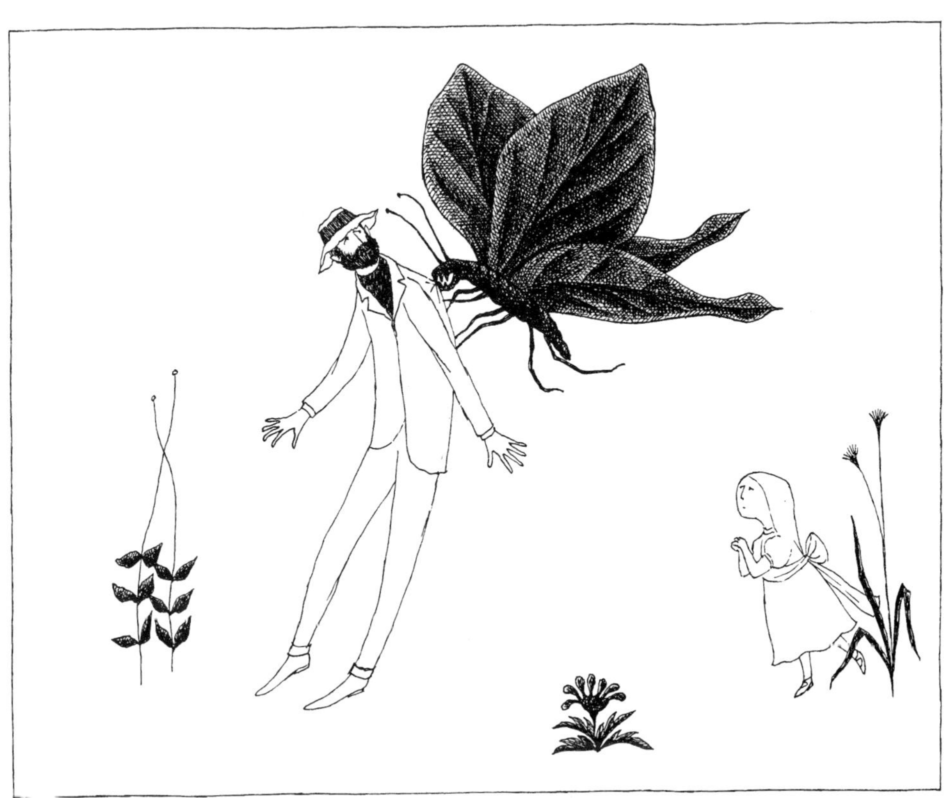

Her sash is lying on the ground,
But Isabelle cannot be found.

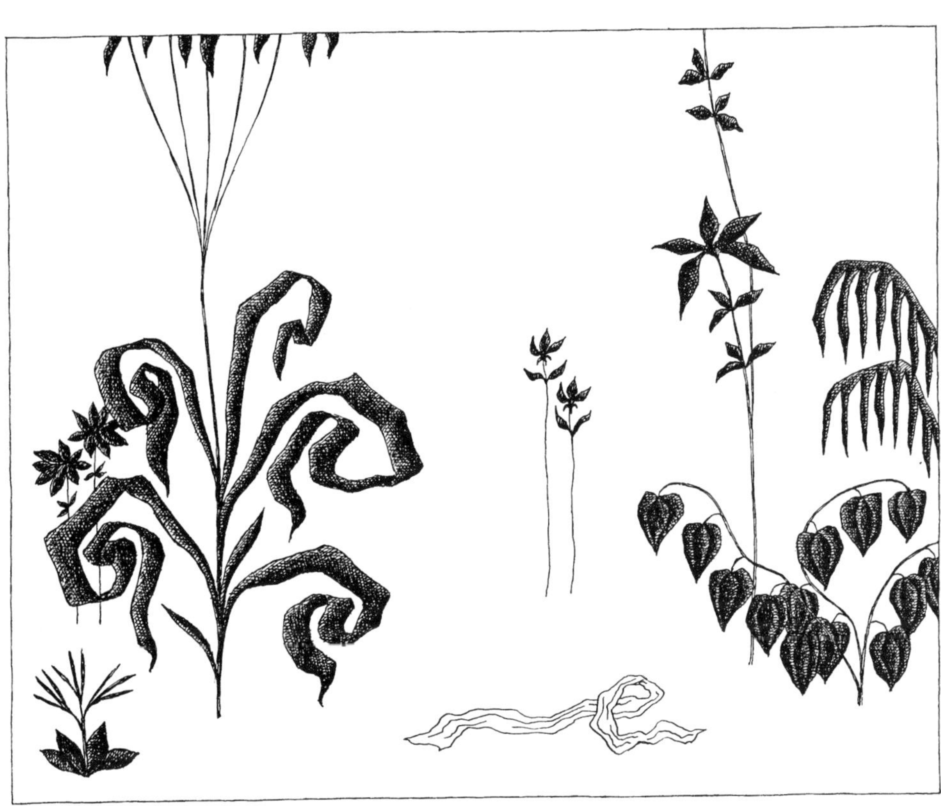

Great-Uncle Franz, beside the lake,
Is being strangled by a snake.

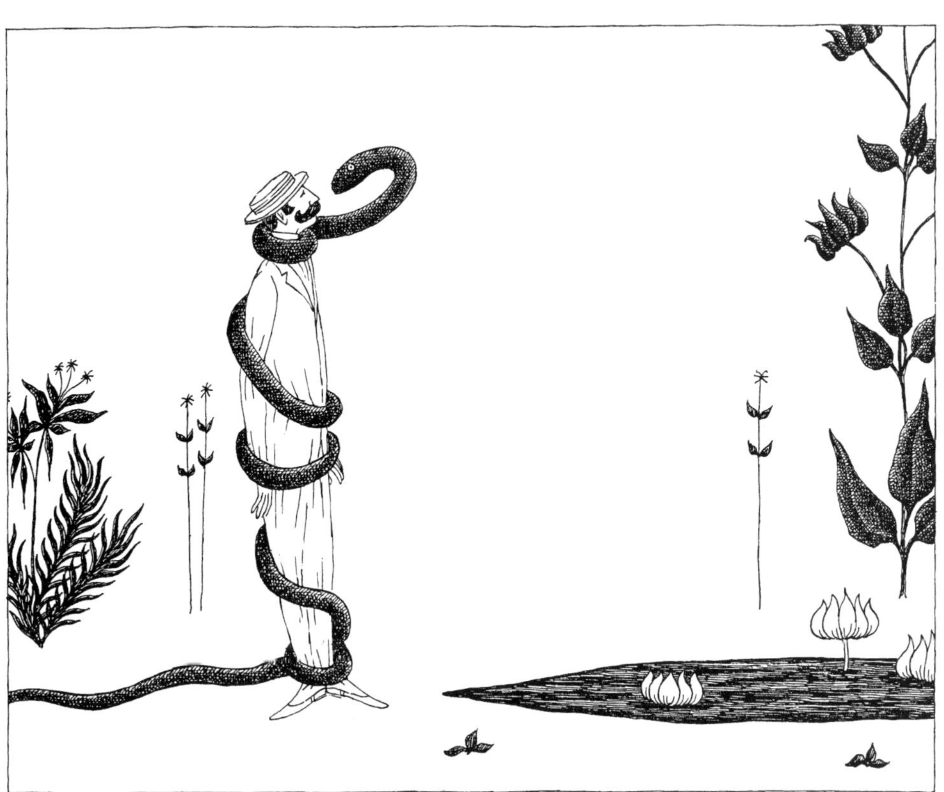

The peaches, apples, plums, and pears
Are guarded by ferocious bears.

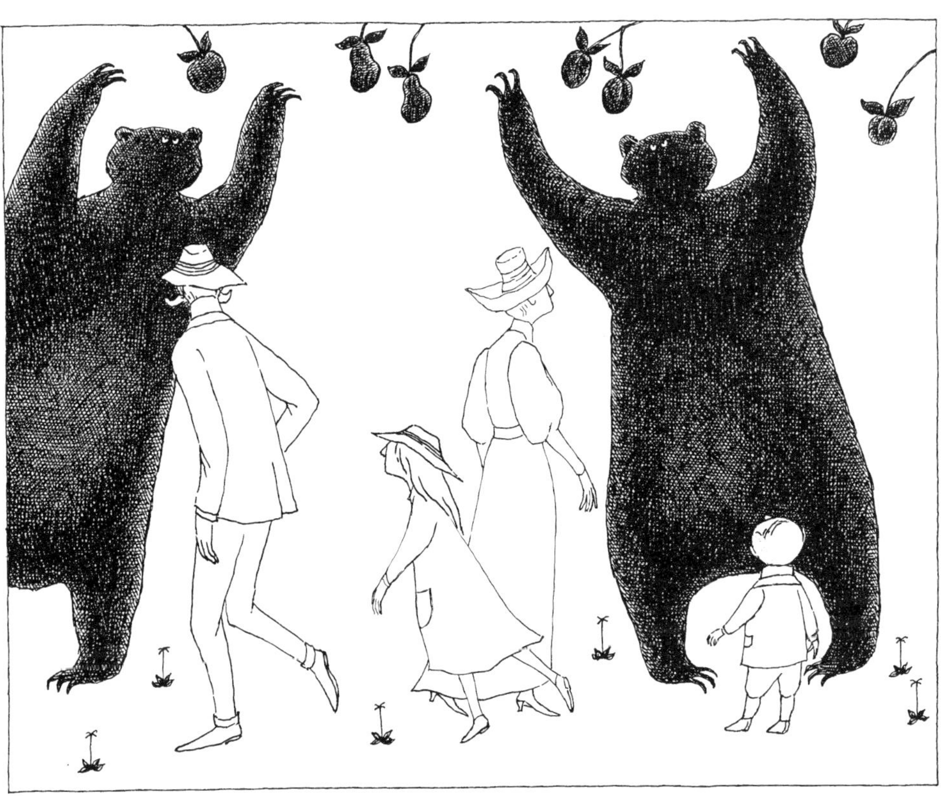

Alexa watches while her aunt
Is pulled feet first inside a plant.

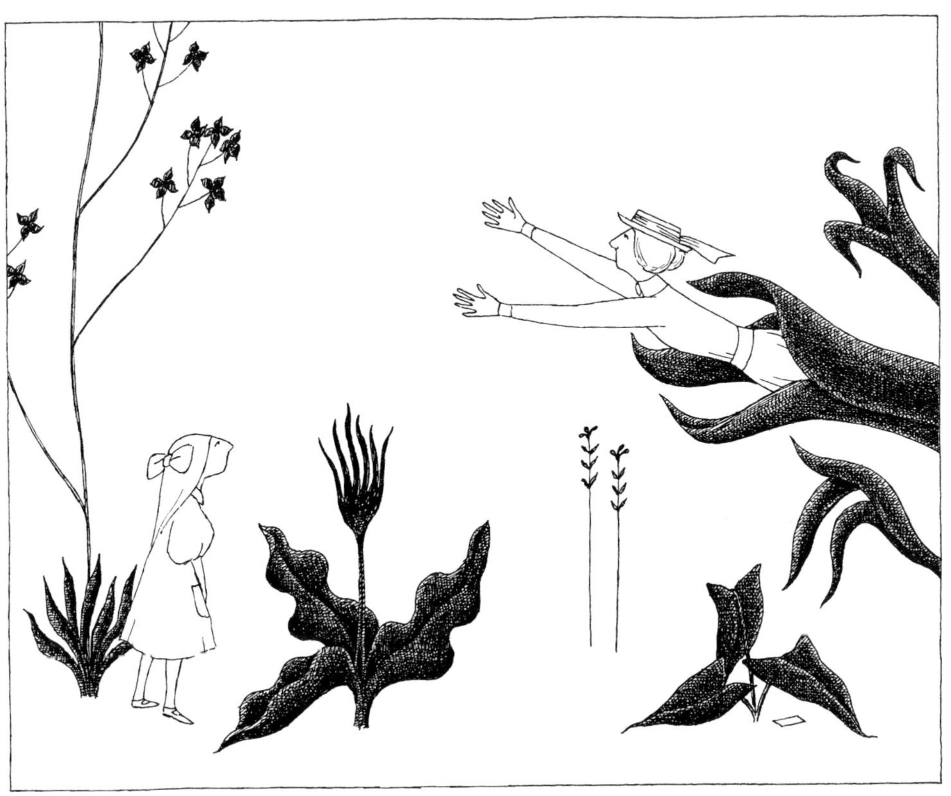

A hissing swarm of hairy bugs
Has got the baby and its rugs.

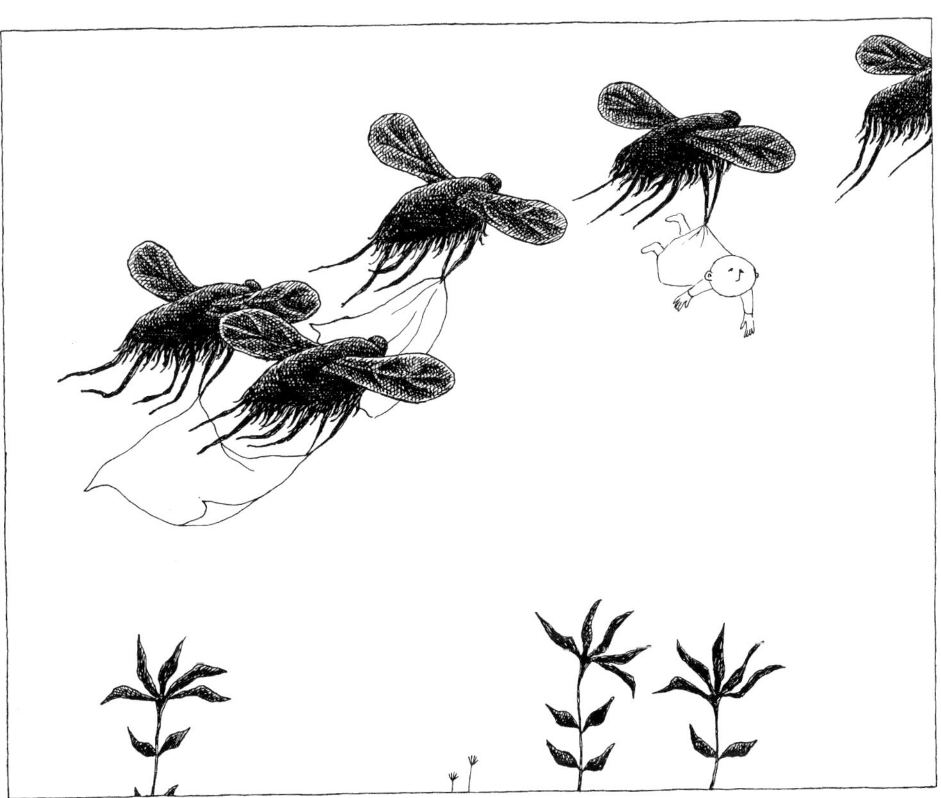

The nurse of whom they all were fond
Is sinking in the bubbling pond.

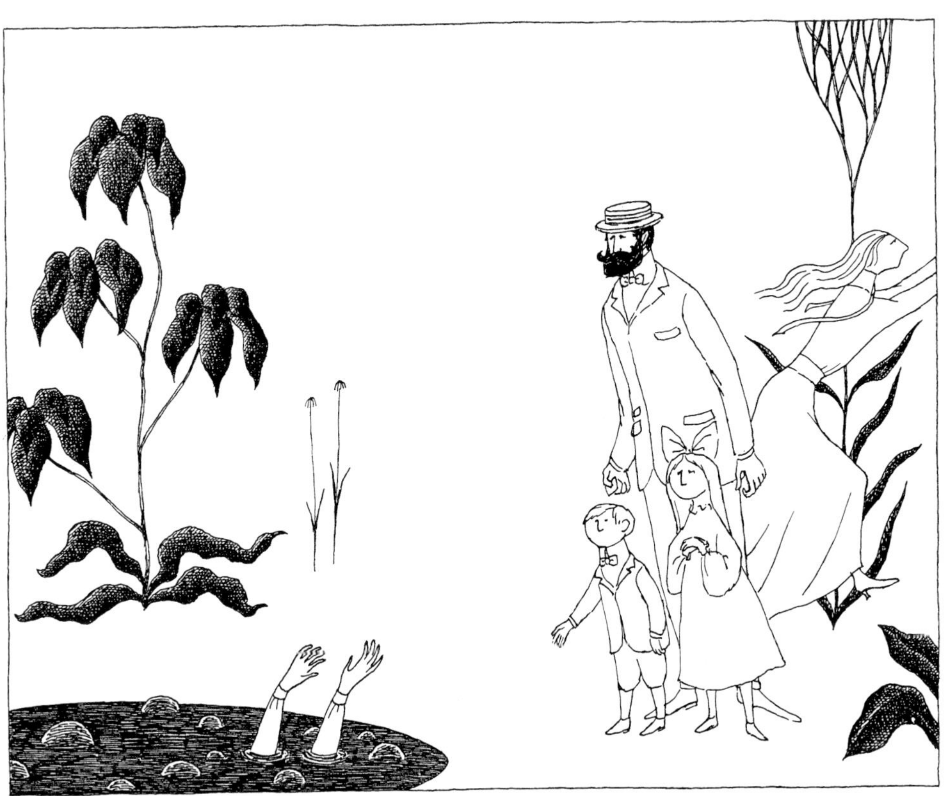

The sky has grown completely black;
It's time to think of turning back.

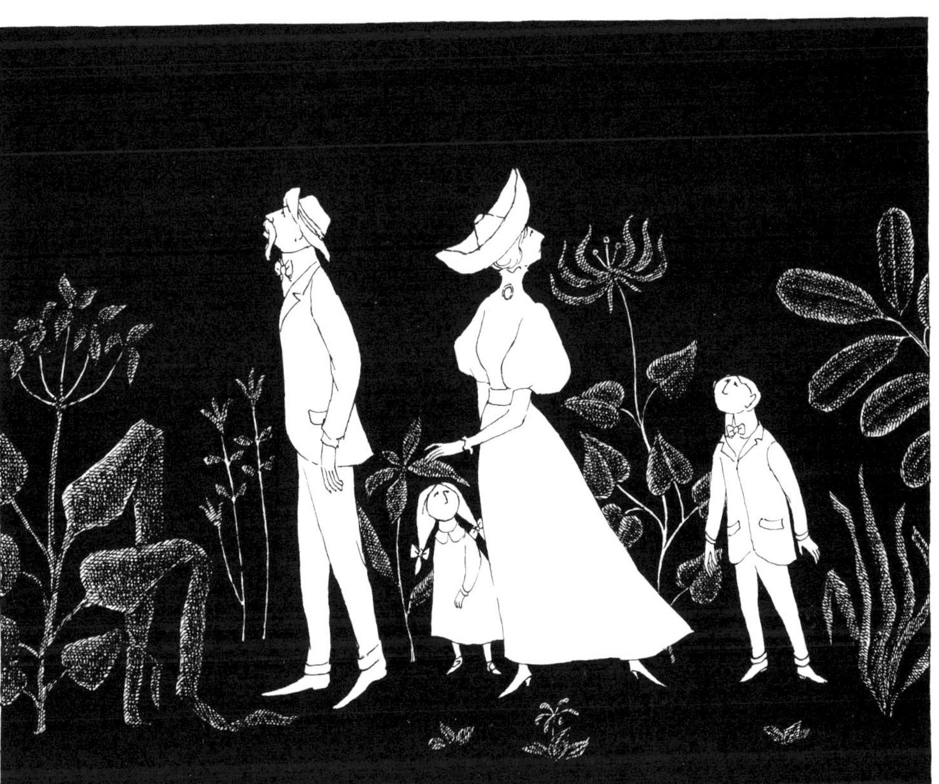

Fall down, or scream, or rush about—
There is no way of getting out.

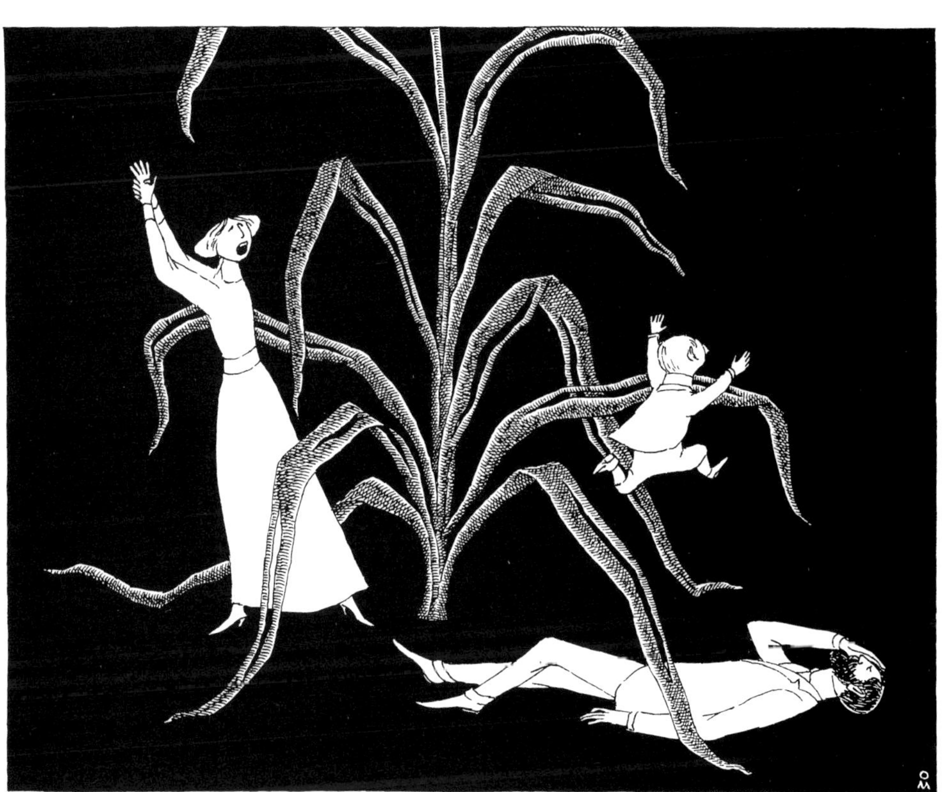

For more Edward Gorey books, puzzles, calendars, games, and stationery, visit pomegranate.com.

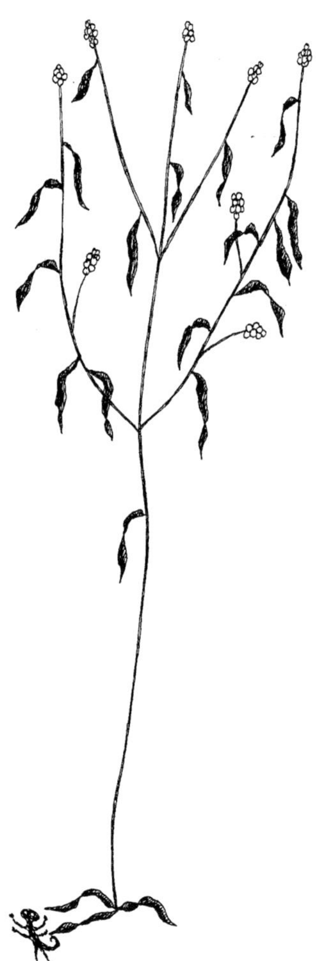

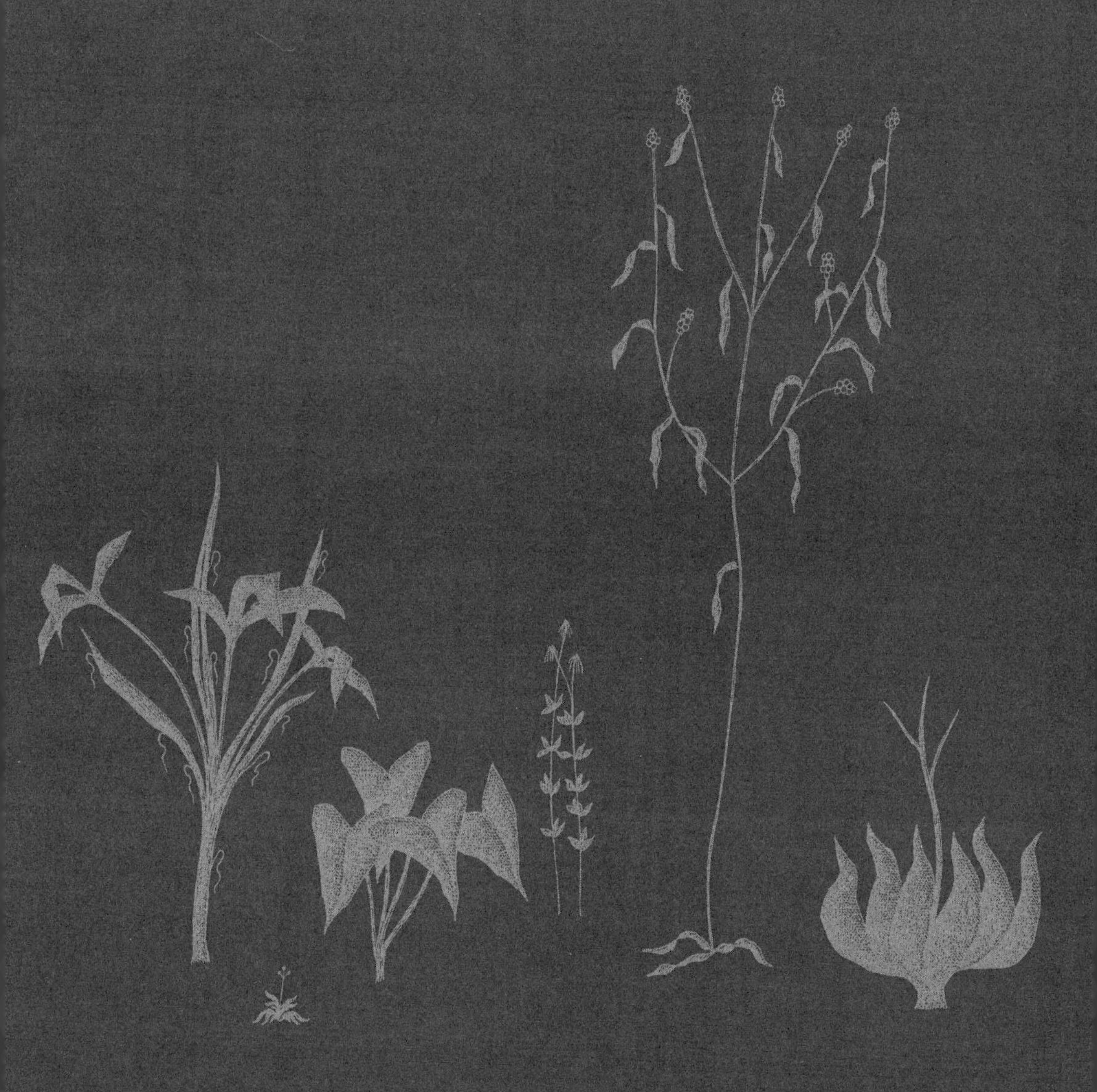